The Lost Kitten

ELVIRA VILLASENOR SHEIKOVITZ

Illustrated by Ronie Pios

Print information available on the last page

Rev. date: 09/25/2015

To order additional copies of this book, contact:
Xlibris
1-888-795-4274
www.Xlibris.com
Orders@Xlibris.com

One weekend morning, Davin goes outside to find out what is making the noise he hears near his bedroom. He finds a kitten shivering under his mother's car. He immediately crawls under the car and picks her up carefully. He holds her tenderly and then brings her inside the house.

Davin shows the kitten to his mother, who is in the kitchen cooking breakfast. She immediately feeds the kitten milk for nourishment. The kitten finishes the milk very fast.

Davin's family nurtures the kitten and names her Hazel because of her green eyes; the cat also has beautiful, white, bushy hair. He takes over the responsibility of caring for her every day. He feeds her and patiently teaches her a lot of tricks, like jumping to catch a hanging rope and chasing birds in the yard. He even teaches Hazel manners, such as sitting when given a command or standing when hearing a whistle.

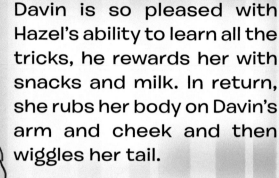

Davin is so pleased with Hazel's ability to learn all the tricks, he rewards her with snacks and milk. In return, she rubs her body on Davin's arm and cheek and then wiggles her tail.

Hazel becomes the center of the family's attention. They all love and pamper her. Emmi, Davin's little sister, feeds her when Davin is not around. Even their little brother, Drew, gives Hazel tender touches and hugs. He also shares his toys as he plays with her.

One Monday morning, Davin and Emmi rush to get ready for school because they have gotten up late. They have to eat breakfast in a hurry. They run out the back door but forget to close it. Their mother is feeding baby Drew, so she does not notice that the door is open.

But Hazel notices. She is curious, so she goes outside and then out to the street. She meets a few street cats, who give her a hard time. Hazel is scared and runs away from them without knowing where she is going.

It is late in the afternoon, and it is raining. Hazel goes up to a house and scratches the front door. The house belongs to Mr. Stanley, who has a son named Dave, who is seven years old. The scratching is loud, so Dave opens the door and sees a wet cat. He immediately takes Hazel into his arms and feeds her.

When Mr. and Mrs. Stanley see Dave with the cat, they are happy that their son has a pet. They name the cat Julie, after Dave's best friend in Texas.

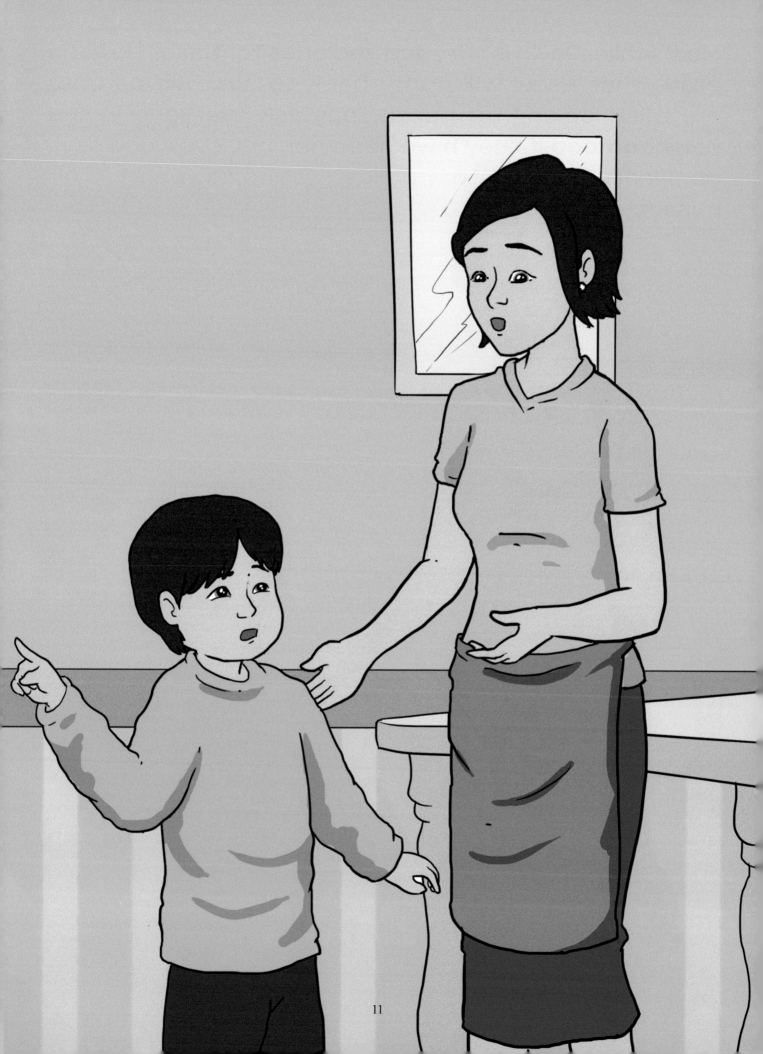

11

Meanwhile, Davin is very sad and cries for Hazel. He even prays that Hazel will come back to him. His parents are busy looking for Hazel. They ask everyone in the neighborhood if they have seen her, but everyone says no. Finally, they go to a police station to report their missing cat.

One Sunday morning, Davin goes to the park where he taught Hazel tricks, and he thinks about the fun they had. While he is sitting on a park bench, two boys pass by him and talk loudly about a cat named Julie. One of the boys is Dave, who proudly tells his friend that he has a beautiful cat, and he talks about her beautiful, white, bushy fur.

As soon as Davin hears this, he joins the conversation and tells Dave that Julie is his missing cat, Hazel. He adds, "I want my cat back."

Dave is embarrassed in front of his friend, and he runs away to tell his father about what happened. Mr. Stanley is very upset and assures Dave that nobody can take Julie away from him.

When Davin's parents hear where Hazel is staying, they go to Dave's house to take Hazel back. But the Stanleys refuse to give up the cat. Without further ado, Davin's parents file a lawsuit against the Stanleys for stealing their cat.

The court summons the Stanleys, the cat, and Dave to appear in court. As soon as they arrive, the court policeman takes the cat. The judge begins the trial by explaining the legality of animal ownership. He asks both Dave and Davin to do something so the cat shows who her real owner is.

Davin presents a trick, and Hazel remembers and jumps out of the policeman's arms and into Davin's arms. Dave cries so hard, and Mr. Stanley hugs him and promises to get him another cat.

The judge watches the emotional reunion of Davin and Hazel, and he also sees that the Stanleys are unhappy. So he immediately rules that both families can have custody of the cat and will have visitation days.

19

Both families agree and are happy. Dave and Davin hug each other with the cat between them.

The End

The End

Printed in the United States
by Baker & Taylor Publisher Services